COOKIE'S CRITTERS
By Cookie Miller

Illustrations done by
Martha Hill and Annabel Crum

Dedicated to God and His wonderful
creation.
For all to enjoy the many creatures
on earth.
And for young readers to learn to read
and enjoy poetry

Contents

THE GREAT SHEPHERD

By Cookie Miller

*Illustration by
Annabel Crum*

THE GREAT SHEPHERD
By Cookie Miller

Jesus is the Great Shepherd.
He loves all His little lambs.
He keeps watch on them.
They are always in His hands.

Lacy was a little lamb,
Who was a part of Jesus' flock.
He loved the meadows and his Mom,
But was about to meet the "Rock".

Lacy ran across the meadows,
Nibbling on sweet grass.
He nibbled here and there,
His tummy was full at last.

But alas, when he looked up,
To find the flock and mother;
He became quite alarmed.
She was gone with all the others.

He knew it was wrong to wander,
His Mom had told him so.
Now he understood her words;
And he didn't know where to go.

He had wondered far away,
The flock were nowhere nearby.
He suddenly was frightened;
And he began to cry.

He knew wolves looked for lambs.
He was alone and felt afraid.
He wondered if the Great Shepherd,
Would hear him if he prayed.

So he cast his eyes toward heaven,
And prayed as best he could;
For help from the Great Shepherd,
And told Him he would be good.

He stood quite still and waited,
As he snubbered back his tears.
Watching across the meadows;
For the Great Shepherd to appear.

There is a good ending to our story;
For as promised in God's Word,
When we ask from hearts sincere,
Ours prayers are always heard.

Jesus, the Shepherd of the flock,
Had heard Lacy when he prayed.
He leaned down and picked up Lacy;
And in Jesus' arms he stayed.

So when you are feeling frightened,
Remember Lacy and his prayer.
When you ask, Jesus will hear you,
You too, will be in God's care.

The End

Spring 2015

A PENGUIN STORY
By Cookie Miller

Illustration By
Annabel Crum

A PENGUIN STORY
By Cookie Miller

When Noah was building the Ark,
He built it where the weather was warm.
Then God called all animals He created,
To the Ark and they did swarm.

Now penguins lived very far away.
They lived where there was ice and snow,
But when they heard God call them,
They knew they had to go!

At first their travels were easy.
For they skated on snow up hill and down.
But as it began to get warmer,
Traveling became harder, they found.

At first there were rivers to swim,
But walking across wide-open plains,
When all they could do was waddle;
Had begun to cause them some pain.

They knew they had to get there.
They knew they must answer God's call.
So they bowed their heads and prayed.
His answer to them they all saw.

Along came other animals,
Whose mission was quite the same.
They too, were on their way to the Ark;
Closer to the penguins they came.

A kangaroo that had an empty pocket,
Picked God's pair of penguins up off the ground;
And dropped them inside her pocket,
Where the penguins felt safe and sound.

Jumping along with the kangaroo,
Was fun as they answered God's call.
Soon their journey was over;
God's blessings had been on them all.

So, when you find life a little scary,
Remember our penguins who trusted the Lord.
Your prayers as well will be covered,
You too, by Him are adored.

The End

12/2015

ZOEY THE ZEBRA
By Cookie Miller

Illustration By
Martha Hill

ZOEY THE ZEBRA
By Cookie Miller

Zoey the Zebra is a very special Zebra.
She was born inside a boat.
It was built by a fellow named Noah;
It was an Ark that God sent afloat.

Noah was a very fine fellow.
The Lord kept him in the palm of His hand.
He worshiped God and followed His Word;
The whole time he walked on the land.

The Bible says God became very upset,
For man was not obeying His Word.
They decided to do what they wanted,
And God's voice to them was not heard.

He had Noah build a mighty Ark;
And take on animals two of a kind.
With God's help the animals came.
There were more than we'd ever find.

Zoey's Mom and Dad were zebras.
They entered the Ark with those who were last.
No sooner had they gotten aboard,
Then the door was shut tight and made fast.

Zoey's Mom had no idea
When she entered the boat,
She would increase their Zebra number,
By having a baby while afloat.

The ship tossed and bounced on the waves.
Zoey's Mom and Dad snuggled close together.
They knew they were in God's hands,
In spite of the wind and the weather.

Sure enough, when time had passed,
When their journey had come to a close;
Not only were there two zebras aboard;
But a third small one with a little pink nose.

An Ark made with God's instructions,
Was a very safe place to be.
And much like the Ark built by Noah,
God offers us something similar, you see.

Your ark little baby Zoey,
Is your Mom and Dad and God's love.
They and he will keep you safe,
For He is watching you all from above.

When times seem to get scary,
When you wonder what life's all about,
Look to God and your Mom and Dad.
All three love you, of that there's no doubt.

A HIPPOPTAMUS
By Cookie Miller

Illustration By
Martha Hill

A HIPPOPTAMUS
By Cookie Miller

Some think a hippopotamus,
A very odd sort of fellow.
With his color a rather dull gray,
Would be better with skin a bright yellow.

But me, I look at the gray,
And think God must have had in mind,
Something that is very special,
Yes, a rare and quite different find.

For God in all of His planning,
Decided that hippos would be as they are.
He hoped we also created by Him,
Would think hippos unequaled by far.

Instead we look at the hippo,
His big clumsy body and feet,
And laugh and giggle right by him;
Not thinking he'll think he's a freak.

But God in Heaven is saddened.
Because we're being so unkind.
God made the hippo different;
To this we're being quite blind.

People are unique like our hippo.
We too, are created by God.
No matter how different we seem,
We're all peas from the same pod.

When we laugh or snicker or giggle,
And someone else starts feeling sad,
Our snickering is the cause of the trouble;
For this we should feel very sad.

So, when you look at a hippo,
Do it with God's heart and mind.
You'll see one wonderful creature,
Because like us, he's one of a kind.

The End

10/26/00

TINY THE TIGER
By Cookie Miller

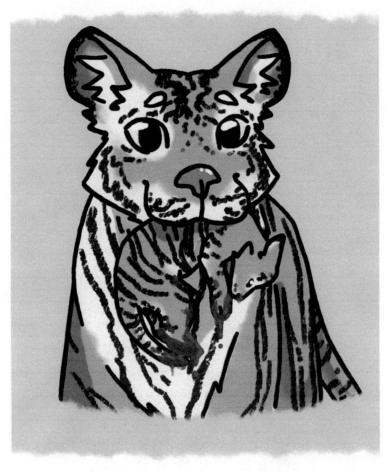

Illustration By
Martha Hill

TINY THE TIGER
By Cookie Miller

Tiny the little tiger,
Found a mud hole his size.
It wasn't very big,
Tiny had found himself a prize.

He pranced right through it,
But when he got only halfway,
His feet would no longer move,
The mud made them stay.

He was stuck where he stood,
And try as he may,
He wasn't sure he'd get out,
Even by the end of the day.

But God was watching,
He had a friend pass on by.
Tiny's orange and black stripes,
Caught his friend's eye.

This friend too, was a tiger,
Much bigger than he,
He picked Tiny up,
His friend's strong teeth were the key.

Tiny's fur at the nape of his neck,
Was thick and held tight.
The big tiger's teeth grabbed him,
Tiny was quite a sight.

Mud dripped from his ankles,
Down onto his toes.
He even had mud,
On the tip of his nose.

All is quite well for Tiny,
His mom washed him real clean.
And Tiny stayed close to home.
He didn't go back to that scene!

From then on he was good.
He decided to stay close to home,
Until he grew much bigger,
And then could safely roam.

So don't you be like Tiny,
And go off on your own.
Be obedient little children,
Stay real close to your home.

You see, God in His heaven,
Is watching from above.
Like Tiny, He wants you to be safe,
And has wrapped you up in His love.

The End

OLLIE THE OCELOT
By Cookie Miller

Illustration By
Martha Hill

OLLIE THE OCELOT
By Cookie Miller

Ocelots have all kinds of spots,
From their head down to their toes.
And if you look close enough,
You can even see some on their nose.

What good are spots on an ocelot,
You are wondering in your head?
Without their spots they could be seen a lot.
Enough I am sure has been said.

Ollie had the usual spots for ocelots,
That kept him safe among the trees.
But alas, one day he heard his Momma say,
"I think your spots flew off in the breeze!"

Now an ocelot without his spots,
Is a sorry sight to see.
So Ollie ran with ocelot speed,
To catch up to that fast moving breeze.

As fast as it was, was not fast enough.
Ollie saw his spots being carried away.
He made one giant leap right into the breeze,
And landed in a big pile of hay.

All of those spots for this young ocelot,
Were no longer flying in the air.
He had to roll in hay most of the day,
To have his spots back in his hair.

It was great that he could run so fast,
For if not, well how awful it would be,
To have an ocelot without his spots,
Spots on ocelots are what keep them free

God our great creator,
Knew what an Ocelot would need.
Besides his many spots to hide,
He also needed much speed.

We, just like Ollie the ocelot,
Are His created beings.
And He, with His great wisdom,
Has given our lives a meaning.

He made us like Him in His image.
He holds us in the palm of His hand.
He loves us with all of His heart,
When we stumble, He understands.

So be grateful you are His creation.
Rejoice that He loves you so much!
Like Ollie you too are uniquely made,
You too, have felt the Master's touch.

The End

PERCY THE POLAR BEAR
By Cookie Miller

Illustration By
Martha Hill

PERCY THE POLAR BEAR
By Cookie Miller

Polar bears look warm and cuddly,
When you see them from far away.
Percy the polar bear was no exception,
If you saw him on any day.

But because he was a polar bear,
Who by nature can be quite mean,
Folks didn't understand,
That Percy came from a different scene.

He loved to be near people,
But they never came close by.
Because he was a polar bear,
They would always run and hide.

So, even though he had other bears,
They just were not the same.
He needed to love people.
I know that sounds rather strange.

God had placed it in his heart,
That hugs and kisses were just great,
Even though he had not done this,
He knew it was his fate.

One day when the sun was shining,
He stepped outside of his lair.
There standing right in front of him,
Was a little boy with dark brown hair.

Percy looked to the right and left.
No one was around.
He slowly walked toward the boy,
And made no growly sound.

The little boy smiled his way.
Percy saw he had no fur, just skin;
It was very cold for furless boys.
He knew just what to give him.

He reached out his paw and drew him near,
What a fun and fuzzy feeling.
Close to Percy the boy felt such warmth,
For Percy it was such a healing.

Suddenly Percy heard a shout.
People saw him with the child.
It looked pretty bad for Percy,
A bear with a boy was pretty wild.

The boy calmly stroked Percy's fur.
He patted him on his head.
Then he slowly walked away.
Nothing more was said.

Those who stood around,
Were awed and realized,
A miracle had just occurred,
Right before their very eyes.

The bear they saw though polar,
Was gentle loving and kind.
The little boy was a friend of Percy's,
This happening was devine.

God's love can reach all hearts,
It changes everything.
Peace, happiness and joy,
Are some of what it brings.

So remember that even polar bears,
Like people can be filled with love.
And when it is sent from our Father,
It comes down from Heaven above.

The End

CHARLIE THE CHEETAH
By Cookie Miller

Illustration By
Martha Hill

CHARLIE THE CHEETAH
By Cookie Miller

On the plains of the Serengeti in Africa,
Many wild animals can easily be seen.
But our story is about a little fellow,
Who I am sure you will think is quite keen.

Charlie the cheetah lived with his family,
Among the tall grasses that swayed in the breeze.
The grasses were the protection for his family.
Staying there for safety was key.

Charlie at first was quite happy.
He didn't know of the world beyond the grass.
Nor did he understand that the cheetah,
When running, could be more than just fast.

As time passed Charlie was growing.
The grass didn't seem nearly as high.
If he stretched his neck he could see,
Other animals as they passed on by.

There was one sight that he spied one day,
A yellow streak that went racing by.
He had not a clue what caused it.
It must be something that has wings and can fly!

There was danger for little cheetahs.
If they wandered out of their hiding place.
Charlie, not knowing the danger,
Found himself on a wide open space.

Suddenly, that golden streak he had seen,
Was heading right straight at him.
He was sure it would not stop.
He found himself in a whirling tail spin.

He stopped spinning rather quickly.
When something grabbed at his neck.
The golden streak turned out to be his father.
Who on the horizon had been just a speck.

That's the day that Charlie learned,
His fate was to be like his father.
He too, would be a yellow streak,
Racing faster than all the others.

That night when curled up by mother,
He dreamed he too, made a streak.
As he raced across the plains of the Serengeti,
He is doing it right now as we speak..

For God has made all His creatures,
That include the likes of you and me.
Being uniquely and wonderful made,
To be all that we were meant to be.

So if ever you feel unworthy,
And want to be different in some silly way,
Remember that you are God's creation,
To be who you are every day.

The End

SCARLETT
By Cookie Miller

Illustration By
Martha Hill

SCARLETT
By Cookie Miller

Deep, deep in the forest,
Among some mighty great trees,
There lived a wee little wolf,
Where all wolves were meant to be free.

Scarlett was a lovely girl wolf,
She was her Daddy's pride.
She always listened and obeyed,
And stayed close by his side.

One day when playing hide and seek,
With the other little wolves,
Scarlett wondered too far to hide.
In a very thick hedge of shrubs.

The other wolf cubs went looking,
But Scarlett could not be found.
Before too long, they grew weary,
And soon they were homeward bound.

Now Scarlett patiently waited,
Deep in the woods among the shrubs.
She had found a great hiding place,
From all the other wolf cubs.

God our Father in heaven,
Cares even for little wolf cubs.
Scarlett was a part of His creation.
He was watching from up above.

Scarlett's father became concerned,
When Scarlett didn't come home.
He knew his little girl cub loved him,
And from him she'd never roam.

So he used his sense of smell,
A gift God gave to many living in the wild.
He started sniffing out her trail.
At first it was light and quite mild.

But before he knew it,
He smelled his girl's scent very strong.
He followed with his nose to the ground,
Knowing he'd find her before long.

Sure enough there was the thicket,
Where Scarlett had hidden for fun.
He growled a soft hello to his girl,
His job of tracking was done.

She was safe within her father's care,
Much like the way God cares for us.
So if you are feeling alone and afraid,
You won't have to make a big fuss.

For you can be assured of this,
God cares much more for you.
He'll answer prayers you ask of Him,
And like Scarlett you'll be care for too!

The End

WILBUR THE WHITE RABBIT
By Cookie Miller

Illustration By
Martha Hill

WILBUR THE WHITE RABBIT
By Cookie Miller

Wilbur was as white as snow.
He lived in a very snowy place.
When one day he found himself,
Running and caught up in a race.

Wilbur, one morning went outside,
To see what he could see.
There across the white, white snow,
Was something strange as could be.

He looked once then looked once again.
There was a rabbit with brown fur.
It flopped its ears and took off,
So fast it became just a blur.

Wilbur took off right after it.
He too, could move quite fast.
But how far could this rabbit run,
Before he would stop at last?

Wilbur started up one hill,
Hopping as fast as he could go.
The brown rabbit stayed ahead of him,
Even though it was very deep snow.

They came upon a frozen lake.
The brown rabbit could not stop,
Until he hit a mound of snow,
And did a giant flop!

Wilbur stopped in front of him.
Said, "Why did you go so fast?"
The brown rabbit looked at Wilbur
Said, "Hopping on snow is a blast!

The snow is soft and I can hop,
High as high can be.
I love the snow. It makes me feel,
As free as free can be."

Wilbur had made a new friend,
For he too, loved the snow.
From that time on and a long time more,
Their friendship began to grow.

So, if you want to make good friends,
Wilbur knows what you should do.
You'll have to stop and say hello,
For many friends, not just a few.

The End

PIMPLES ON AN ELEPHANT
By Cookie Miller

Illustration By
Martha Hill

PIMPLES ON AN ELEPHANT
By Cookie Miller

Georgie was quite beautiful.
That's what his Momma said.
Even though he was all wrinkles,
From his toes up to his head.

For wrinkles on an elephant,
Are just what God designed,
So, Georgie and other elephants,
Thought wrinkles were just fine.

But pimples on an elephant,
That can be a tragic thing.
Georgie would sadly tell you,
Of the troubles it can bring.

The first pimple that appeared,
Was very very small.
It was just a little pink thing,
That caused no concern at all.

The second pimple was much larger,
Where other elephants could see.
It grew big and pink and bumpy,
In the center of Georgie's knee.

"So what," you say, "a pimple,
On a little elephant's knee,
Could not really be a problem,
Cause elephants don't climb trees."

That's true a second pimple,
Amounted to not much.
But then a third and fourth appeared,
And they were tender to the touch.

Momma, still not too concerned,
Had Georgie eat alfalfa grass.
This just made those pimples grow,
Much larger and quite fast.

Pinker and much closer,
Together they did grow.
The lovely gray an wrinkled look,
On Georgie, began to go.

He now looked pink and bumpy.
More pimples did appear.
They even were more visible,
On the tips of Georgie's ears.

A pink elephant! Poor Georgie,
A lumpy one at best.
From gray and wrinkled to pink and bumpy,
Georgie was quite different from the rest.

Momma's elephant's friends and neighbors,
Were sympathetic to say the least.
But Georgie's friends would snicker,
Unkind comments soon increased.

Georgie became very lonely.
With him, no one wanted to play.
He had no one to talk too,
When he had something to say.

The little elephants wandered into the jungle,
Far away from their Momma's care.
Georgie followed far behind them,
Cause he knew they would stare.

The jungle became much thicker,
Darker, dense, and deep.
Georgie became frightened,
His friends began to shriek.

They realized they had gone too far.
They were lost and couldn't get back.
The darkness of the jungle seemed darker,
They knew they had gone off the track.

In the evening with dinner time close,
The Mommas were trumpeting their calls,
But no little elephants came running,
No gray wrinkled or pink pimpled a all.

The Pappa elephants heard the honking.
They came running. All were alarmed.
For they knew with all this commotion,
Someone could be seriously harmed.

"Please go hurry and find them.
Our babies are lost in the trees."
The Momma elephants pleaded,
"They are cold and might even freeze!"

The Poppas left out a loud trumpet call.
For sure the little elephants would hear.
If they hadn't wondered off too far,
The calls would sound in their ears.

Georgie standing in the darkness,
Was pink and a bright shining light.
For all the pimples on his hide,
Instead of dull gray were very bright.

The other youngster elephants,
Decided pink on an elephant not bad.
Cause the bright pink pimply Georgie,
In the jungle was all they had.

They heard trumpet calls in the distance,
As they stood watching their lovely pink friend.
The trumpet sounds kept getting closer,
Their scary journey had come to an end.

The Poppa elephants saw a light,
It was Georgie's lovely pink hide.
And all the other little elephants,
Were standing there right by his side.

Moral to this story?
I'll make it very clear.
It doesn't matter how you look,
Or even what you wear.

For often when you least expect,
The things you do not like,
Can be the very thing to help,
When the spot you're in is tight.

The End

SNOWFLAKE
By Cookie Miller

Illustration By
Annabel Crum

SNOWFLAKE
By Cookie Miller

Some cats are gray, some cats are black.
Some are even multicolored.
But snowflake was especially rare.
She was quite different from all others.

You see, her fur was as white as snow,
And as soft as soft can be.
Although this was a gift from God,
Snowflake wanted all to see.

Because she was so beautiful,
She thought she was better than others.
She didn't like all the other cats,
Even the ones that were her brothers.

She kept her nose up in the air,
Whenever they were around.
She just kept tending to her fur,
And didn't make a sound.

Until one day an alley cat,
All full of dirt and grit,
Came running past her pillow,
And on it he did sit.

Snowflake was quite upset,
How dare he such a fellow.
If she sat upon her pillow now,
Her fur might turn all yellow.

He probably had awful fleas,
As he sat upon her pillow,
How thoughtless and uncaring,
This dirty alley cat fellow.

It didn't cross Snowflake's mind,
That she should share with this cat.
She didn't think about his need,
Poor cat didn't even own a mat.

Someone poor and homeless,
That was the alley cat's fate.
He saw Snowflake's lovely pillow,
And thought that it was great!

Snowflake's brothers saw the alley cat,
They knew he was in need.
They thought Snowflake was being kind.
How surprised they were indeed.

They told Snowflake she was kind.
The thought for her was new.
She kind of liked what she heard,
And let them think that it was true.

The alley cat got up to go,
Snowflake told him he could stay.
She discovered it felt pretty good,
To do a good deed on this day.

Suddenly, how she looked,
And how white and soft her fur,
Was no longer something she cared about.
She wanted caring to be part of her.

It felt so good, much better,
Then looking proud and white.
For Snowflake on this special day,
Found that kindness was just right.

Moral of the story is,
To be kind and spread God's love.
When we care for each other,
God sends us joy from up above.

The End

LARRY THE LION
By Cookie Miller

Illustration By
Martha Hill

LARRY THE LION
By Cookie Miller

Larry the Lion was mighty,
When he growled the whole jungle knew,
That Larry was very angry,
All took notice, not just a few.

He would lift his head and roar,
Then shake his mighty mane.
He scared the other animals,
But he felt no shame.

One day as he was roaring,
And shaking his mighty mane,
He and others noticed hair flying,
Into the air and across the plain.

No matter Larry thought,
His mane was very thick,
Maybe if he didn't shake as much,
That would do the trick.

For you see Larry, if he lost his mane,
Would be a funny sight,
He just couldn't do without his mane.
He'd look an awful fright.

Larry's mane kept losing hair,
No matter what he tried,
Till finally there was no mane at all,
And he began to hide.

While Larry hid away by himself,
He had time to think and understand,
That all that roaring he had done,
Had caused problems in jungle land.

He began to feel quite bad,
If only he had his mane,
He'd go back and tell his friends,
He really was ashamed.

Yes, God is good even to lions,
Who frighten all their friends,
Larry's mane grew back again,
Our story has a happy end.

Larry did his roaring still,
He is a lion you see,
But now his roar is a warning,
Without anger, that's the key.

God is quite happy too,
For the lesson Larry learned,
It's one we should remember as well,
God's delight is what we'll earn.

YUM YUM YAMMA LEAVES
By Cookie Miller

Illustration By
Annabel Crum

YUM YUM YAMMA LEAVES
By Cookie Miller

Lionel loves nibbling on tender leaves from a Yamma tree.
Being a young giraffe and not very tall, he couldn't reach
up high enough to get youngest and most tender leaves.

Every morning Lionel ran along with the other giraffes
in the herd, staying close to his mother.

When he found a Yamma tree that looked promising,
he stretched his neck and then stretched his long
tongue even farther. Still unable to reach the tender
leaves, he stretched some more and reached some more

until he had an awful kink in his neck. His tongue became
so dry that he could hardly stand it. He looked
over at his mother and the other giraffes.
They were intently chewing away. Lionel was not happy.

One morning Lionel decided he was going to find a tree
his own size. While the others chewed on their Yamma leaves,
he wandered away. He looked for what seemed like hours
until suddenly, there it was, the perfect tree.
It was just a little taller than he had hoped but there were
many tender little leaves well within reach.

Lionel began chewing immediately. He chewed awhile
and stretched his long neck awhile.

He worked his head up toward one limb and
around another. He chewed and chewed and chewed.
He stretched a little farther and twisted his neck
a little more and chewed some more.

Suddenly he was startled by a lot of squawking.
His ear had twitched and practically knocked
a bird's nest out of the tree, mother bird, babies and all.
Lionel was so intent on chewing his Yamma leaves
he hadn't noticed the nest.
He felt awfully bad about scaring them.
He tried to back away only to discover
that his neck was stuck.
He tilted his head and twisted his neck this way and that,
but he could not get free.
He was hopelessly trapped in the branches of his
perfect sized Yamma tree.

Mr. Wallace, the game warden, was out on his rounds
checking the game preserve where Lionel
and his family lived. He had stopped by his
friend Joey's house to see if he would like to ride along.
Joey rarely turned down the opportunity.
Occasionally he Mr. Wallace would let him help
rescue a babyanimal that had gotten into trouble.

"Poor little giraffe," Mr. Wallace said to Joey, as he
rounded a bend and saw Lionel caught in the
tree. The mother bird was dive bombing Lionel's head
and squawking frantically. Lionel looked very sad.

Mr. Walllace and Joey climbed out of the jeep
to survey the situation. They stood back and looked.

They walked slowly around the tree and looked again,
trying to see how they could help. "Well Joey,"
Mr. Wallace said, "We could try cutting branches
off the tree, but the birds would not have shade.
Besides, a saw makes a lot of noise and would shake
the tree. I think the birds and our
little giraffe have been frightened enough. We will
have to think of something else."

Joey slowly walked over to Lionel and patted his neck.
He talked to him softly. "Don't worry little fellow.
We will get you out of here." Lionel looked
pleadingly at him with his big brown eyes,
all moist from the tears he had been shedding.

Joey tried pulling on Lionel's neck while Mr. Wallace
pushed down on his head. That didn't work.
Lionel's jaws were too wide. Then Mr. Wallace tried
bending a branch or two. That didn't work either.

Lionel was too entangled. Mr. Wallace and Joey
stepped back to look over the situation again.

Suddenly, Joey's eyes lit up. He said, "You know
Mr. Wallace, this reminds me of the time when
my Mom had a ring stuck on her finger.
It was too small.
She put butter all over her finger and the
ring popped right off." "Joey, that is a wonderful
idea," Mr. Wallace said as he headed for his jeep.
"I have some cooking oil in my jeep from my last
camping trip. We will try it."

Joey and Mr. Wallace smoothed cooking oil all over
Lionel's neck and jaws. Then they pulled
and tugged and pushed until suddenly, "POP"!
Just like Joey's mother's ring, Lionel's head
came loose,
then his neck, and there he was, free at last!

The mother bird and babies were chirping happily.
Mr. Wallace and Joey were smiling. Lionel was
jumping for joy.

He could run and twist his neck and bend over
to eat the grass and reach leaves on lower
branches and....oh how good those leaves on lower
branches tasted now!

Mr. Wallace said, "Come on Joey. Let's see about
getting this little fellow back to his herd.
It will soon be time to get you home too."

Lionel had a lot to tell his mother. He had
learned there was safety in staying near her.
He knew someday he would be tall enough
to reach those
Yamma leaves that were up so high, but
he decided he could wait for them until he was tall
enough to reach them.

THE END

Made in United States
Troutdale, OR
10/18/2024